JUDY MOODY AND FRIENDS

One, Two, Three, ROAR!

Megan McDonald

illustrated by Erwin Madrid

based on the characters
created by Peter H. Reynolds

CANDLEWICK PRESS

CONTENTS

BOOK 1

Jessica Finch in Pig Trouble   1

BOOK 2

Rocky Zang in The Amazing Mr. Magic   65

BOOK 3

Amy Namey in Ace Reporter   129

Jessica Finch
in Pig Trouble

For Ashley

M. M.

For my nieces, Melanie and Mariel

E. M.

CONTENTS

CHAPTER 1

Just Say *Oink* 5

CHAPTER 2

This Little Piggy 23

CHAPTER 3

The PeeGee WeeGee Club 47

CHAPTER 1
Just Say *Oink*

Pigs, pigs, and more pigs! Jessica
Finch loved pigs.

Jessica Finch had a dream. A big
pig dream. She dreamed of having a
pet pig.

If she had a pig, they would read
books together. And ride bikes. And
have sleepovers.

Jessica called her friend Judy Moody. "Emergency," she told Judy. "Come right away."

Judy Moody rode her bike up the hill to Jessica's house.

"I came as fast as I could," said Judy. "What's the emergency?"

"It's a pig emergency," said Jessica Finch.

"RARE!" Judy said.

"Come on," said Jessica, and Judy
followed her upstairs to her room.

Jessica's room was pink. Pink, pinker, pinkest. Pinker than bubble gum. Pink as a pig's tail. And her room was full of . . . pigs. Pig books. Pig pillows. Pig posters. Piggy banks. Even a fuzzy piggy-face rug.

"Your room is one big pigpen!" said Judy.

"Thanks!" said Jessica. She glanced out into the hall. She closed her door. She made her voice almost a whisper.

"Okay. So. You know how it's almost my birthday, right?"

"Right! Happy *almost* birthday," said Judy.

"And you know how there's only one thing I want for my birthday, right? More than anything else in the whole world."

"Umm . . . a piggy cake?" asked Judy.

"No. Not a piggy cake.

Not a piggy coin purse.

Not a piggy clock.

Just one single present. A real-live, cute-as-a-button, potbellied pig."

Judy's eyes grew as big as gum balls.

"Potbellied pigs are super cute and super smart and super cuddly," said Jessica. "And I dropped a million and one hints, like telling my parents that my birthday just happens to be on the same day as National *Pig* Day."

"Really?"

"Really."

"Happy *almost* Pig Day, too," said
Judy. "But I think you have about a million
in one chance of getting a real live P-I-G.
You might as well ask for an aardwolf."

"A-A-R-D-W-O-L-F," said Jessica
Finch, Super Speller.

"So what's the emergency anyway?"
Judy asked.

"Right. You have to help me snoop
around. I just have to know if I'm getting
a P-I-G."

"Judy Moody, Super Snoop, at your
service. Where do we start?"

13

Jessica squinted her eyes. Jessica pinched up her face, thinking. "I know!" she said. "Under my mom and dad's bed."

"You think there might be a pig under your mom and dad's bed?" Judy asked.

Jessica Finch snorted. "No, see, we snoop for normal presents. If we find any, that's bad. If we don't find any, that's good."

Judy scrunched up her face. "How is *no* presents a good thing?"

"If we don't find presents, I just know I'm getting a real pig. If we find normal presents, no pig."

Judy just shrugged. She had no pig sense at all.

"Come on. I know all the good hiding places," said Jessica. "You be my lookout."

"Roger," said Judy.

"Who's Roger?"

"Never mind," said Judy.

"If you hear footsteps, just say *oink*," Jessica told Judy. "One oink for Mom. Two oinks for Dad."

"Gotcha," said Judy.

Jessica took Judy's arm and dragged her down the hall.

Jessica looked under the bed.

Jessica looked in
the window seat.

Jessica went to
look in the closet.

"Oink! Oink!" Judy was oinking!

"Who? What? Where?" asked Jessica.

"I think I heard footsteps," said Judy.

Jessica listened at the top of the stairs. Quiet. Dead quiet. "I don't hear anything," she said.

"Sorry," said Judy. "False-alarm oink."

Jessica opened the closet door. She stood on a box. She pulled down a bag. *Crunch, crunch, crunch* went the paper. Jessica's heart sank.

"Oh, no!"

"What's wrong?" Judy asked.

"I found presents," said Jessica.

She peered into the bag. "A piggy flashlight. An I ♥ Piggies notebook. Even a game called Pig Out. That means no potbellied pig."

"Oink," said Judy.

"Ratday," said Jessica, slumping down on the bed.

"Huh?"

"It's Latin. Pig Latin for *drat*."

CHAPTER 2
This Little Piggy

Jessica Finch was ummedbay outway. B-U-M-M-E-D O-U-T.

Judy tried to cheer her up. "Let's play the game," Judy whispered.

"What game?"

"The Pig Out game!" said Judy.

"Now? But it's for my birthday. My mom will get mad."

"We'll just play it once," said Judy. "C'mon. It'll be upersay unfay."

"Super fun! Then we put it back and nobody will know?" said Jessica.

"They don't call me Super Snoop for nothing," said Judy.

Jessica perked up. She ran back inside, grabbed the game, and then ran back to her room.

In no time, Jessica and Judy sat crisscross applesauce on the fuzzy pink piggy rug.

"So, how do you play?" asked Judy.

Jessica tore the lid off of the box.
"There's no board. You just roll the five
little piggies like dice," said Jessica Finch,
Pig Expert. "And you get points for how
they land." She showed Judy the score
chart.

Judy rolled the pigs. "Snorter! Ten points!"

Jessica rolled the pigs. "Side of bacon! Minus ten points!"

Judy rolled the pigs again.

One landed on top of another.

"Pig pyramid!" yelled Jessica.

"Is that good?"

"Good? That's fifty points!" said
Jessica. "You win."

"Play again?" Judy begged.

"Shh," said Jessica. "Did you hear that?"

"Hear what?"

Somebody was coming up the stairs.

"Quick! Hide the pigs!" Jessica whispered.

Judy shoved the pigs under the rug. Jessica hid the box under her bed.

Mrs. Finch walked past Jessica's room. Mrs. Finch went down the hall into the bathroom.

"Phew. That was close," said Jessica. "I better put this back."

"And I better go home," said Judy. "Before we get in *pig* trouble."

Jessica and Judy laughed like hyenas.

"Are you sure you have to go?"

"Yep. I have to feed the . . . um . . . my Venus flytrap."

As soon as Judy was gone, Jessica put the game back in the box. "One little, two little, three little, four little piggies—" Uh-oh! Piggy Number Five was issingmay! Missing!

Jessica looked under her leg. She looked under the rug.

She looked under the bed.

NTBF! Nowhere To Be Found.
Pig-a-ma-jig!

Jessica Finch ran out of the house and hopped on her super-pink bike. She rode super fast to Judy Moody's house. She honked her Super Pig bike horn all the way up the driveway to the Moody backyard.

Jessica took off her helmet. She heard noises coming from a blue tent in the backyard. A tent with a sign that said T. P. CLUB.

"Knock, knock," called Jessica.

Judy poked her head out of the tent flap.

"Do you know where my pig is?" Jessica asked Judy.

Judy's eyes bugged out. "Pig? What pig?"

"One of the little plastic piggies is missing. From the Pig Out game."

"Oh, *that* pig," said Judy.

Pee! Gee! Wee! Gee!

Jessica heard a strange sound. She looked around. "Hey, what was that sound?"

"What sound? I didn't hear a sound."

Pee! Gee! Wee! Gee!

"There it is again. A squeak. A high-pitched squeak."

"Maybe it was a mouse," said Judy.

"It was louder than a mouse."

"I mean, maybe it was Mouse. My cat."

"Your cat's in there?"

"Sure. Why not?"

Jessica shrugged. Then she heard the sound again.

Pee! Gee! Wee! Gee!

"There. Didn't you hear *that*?"

"Squeaky door," said Judy.

"But your tent doesn't have a door," said Jessica. Sometimes Judy Moody was one oink short of a litter.

"Then it must be Stink," said Judy. "Squeaky Stink."

"Your little brother's in there, too?"

"Sure. Why not?"

"Well, can I come in?" said Jessica.

"NO!" said Judy. "I mean, no."

Stink popped his head out of the tent, too. He pointed to the word *CLUB* on the sign. "Members only," he said.

"Yeah, sorry. Those are the rules," said Judy.

"But I never get to be in your clubs. Can't I be in your club? Just this once? For my birthday?"

Judy shook her head. "Rules are rules," she said.

"Atray inkfay," said Jessica.

"I am not a rat fink," said Judy.

Jessica Finch made a pinch face. Jessica Finch felt like she might cry.

"Judy Moody, you are not a friend. You are not even a Super Snoop. You are just . . . a big . . .

M-E-A-N-I-E!"

Jessica Finch stomped away. She stomped across the grass. She stomped down the sidewalk. She hopped on her bike and sped all the way home. She did not look back once.

"MOM!" she yelled when she got back home.

"Kitchen," her mom called.

"Judy Moody is my UN-friend. She is UN-invited to my parties."

"But, honey, you already asked her," said her mom.

"Then I will UN-ask her."

D-R-A-T! National Pig Day was about to become National Rat Day.

CHAPTER 3
The PeeGee WeeGee Club

At last it was March first. Jessica Finch's birthday. National Pig Day! The only thing missing was one perfect pet potbellied pig.

Jessica Finch had not one, but two parties: an after-school piggy party and a next-Sunday bowling party. Jessica Finch had a piggy cake and pink ice cream with her friends Rocky, Frank, and Amy Namey. NOT with Judy Moody.

Jessica Finch opened piggy presents.

Jessica Finch and her friends played Pig Out—minus one piggy.

"Happy Birthday!" said Amy.

"You don't seem very happy," said Frank.

"Yeah, why are you such a Debbie Downer today?" asked Rocky.

Just then, Jessica Finch heard a sound. A high-pitched squealing sound—*Pee! Gee! Wee! Gee!*—coming from right outside her very own house!

"It's that sound again!" Jessica said. "You guys hear that, right?"

"What sound?" said Rocky and Frank at the same time.

"I don't hear anything," said Amy,
but she couldn't help giggling.

Jessica ran down the hall. *Was she out of her peegee-weegee mind?*

She ran to the front door. She peeked out the window. *Judy Moody?*

"Go away, Udyjay Oodymay!" she called.

"Just open the door," said Rocky and Frank.

"Yes, just open the door," said Amy.

Jessica Finch crossed her arms. Jessica Finch turned her back to her friends.

Jessica Finch did not open the door.

"Jessica, open the door," said her mom.

"Let Judy in," said her dad.

Rat fink! Even her parents were being pig heads.

Jessica Finch cracked open the door. "I'm still mad at you," she told Judy through the crack.

Pee! Gee! Wee! Gee!

There it was again. That sound! Louder than ever!

Jessica Finch flung open the door.

There was Judy, holding a lumpy
yellow baby blanket in her arms. And
curled up in the lumpy yellow baby
blanket was . . . a cute-as-a-button,
perfect, potbellied piglet!

It had fuzzy pink legs, fuzzy gray
polka-dot spots, and a curly pink tail.

It even had a big pink bow tied around its head.

"*Pee! Gee! Wee! Gee!*" went the piggy.

Jessica Finch squealed and jumped up and down.

Judy handed over the squirmy bundle of pig. "He's from your mom and dad," she said.

"Happy Birthday, honey," said her parents at the same time.

Jessica Finch could not believe her eyes. Jessica Finch could not believe her ears, arms, or elbows.

"Thank you, thank you, thank you, Mom and Dad," said Jessica. "But how? Where? I looked everywhere. When did you—"

"He was hiding at *my* house!" squealed Judy.

"We asked Judy to take care of the little guy for a few days," said Jessica's mom.

"Judy Moody, Pig Sitter, at your service," said Judy.

"Ohh! That's why you wouldn't let me in the tent!" said Jessica.

"Sorry I acted like a weenie," Judy said.

"Sorry I called you a meanie," Jessica said.

"Pee! Gee! Wee! Gee!" said the little piglet.

Jessica A. Finch's very own
potbellied pig.

"He's perfect!" she said.

"I know. Let's have a piggy party!"

Jessica and her friends played
with the new piggy. They fed him
baby cereal . . .

and goat's milk.

They played with a squeaky toy,

a ball,

and a stuffed cat.

"What are you going to name him?" asked Jessica's mom.

"How about Mr. Piggles," said Amy.

"Oinkers," said Judy.

"Sir Squeals-a-Lot," said Frank.

"Norman Vincent Pig," said Rocky.

Jessica needed a perfect name for the most perfect pig in all the world.

"Pee! Gee! Wee! Gee!" said the pig.

"I'm going to name you PeeGee WeeGee," said Jessica. "And I'm starting a new club. The PeeGee WeeGee Club!"

"Uh-oh," said Judy.

"Uh-oh is right," said Frank. He wiped his hands down the sides of his pants. "What do we have to do to be in the club?"

"You just have to be able to say *PeeGee WeeGee!*" said Jessica.

"PEEGEE WEEGEE!" everybody shouted.

PeeGee WeeGee curled his tail right around Jessica's little pinky finger.

"He curled his tail!" said Jessica. "I bet that means he's happy."

If Jessica had a pig tail, she would have curled it, too. Jessica A. Finch was in Pig Heaven!

Rocky Zang in
The Amazing Mr. Magic

For the original Rocky Zang

M. M.

For my brother, Edward,
and sister-in-law, Pitchie

E. M.

CONTENTS

CHAPTER 1

The Amazing Mind Reader 69

CHAPTER 2

The Best Backyard Magic Show Ever 87

CHAPTER 3

The Disappearing Dollar 111

CHAPTER 1
The Amazing Mind Reader

Abracadabra! Kalamazoo!

Rocky had a magic wand. Rocky had a black top hat. Rocky had a long, dark cape. Meet the Amazing Mr. Magic!

Rocky could make a hankie change colors. Rocky could make a flower appear out of thin air. Rocky could make his very own thumb fly across the room.

The Amazing Mr. Magic was *almost* ready for the Best Backyard Magic Show Ever. The last thing he needed was one really good card trick. The Vanishing Ace? The Floating Joker? *Aha!* The Amazing Mind Reader!

Just then, his across-the-street best friend, Judy Moody, rode her bike down the sidewalk. *Alla kazam!* He could practice the trick on her.

"Hey, Judy. Pick a card," said Rocky. "Any card. But don't tell me what it is!"

"Okay," said Judy. "Now what?"

"Now put the card back."

Judy put the card back.

"Now I'm going to mix the cards all up. Then I'll read your mind and pull your card from the deck. Prepare to be amazed."

Rocky shuffled the cards.
Rocky closed his eyes. Rocky said,
"Hocus pocus, Jiminy bebop."

"Are those *real* magic words?" Judy asked.

"Shh. The Amazing Mr. Magic needs quiet to read your mind." Rocky pulled a card from the middle of the deck.

"Was it the ace of spades?"

"Nope. The queen of hearts," said Judy.

"Rats," said Rocky. "Try again?"

"Okay." Judy picked another card and put it back.

Rocky shuffled the deck.

Rocky closed his eyes.

He said the magic words.

Rocky pulled out a card.

"The jack of diamonds?" asked
Rocky.

"Nope. The two of clubs."

"Double rats," said Rocky.

He tried one more time. "The nine
of hearts?" asked Rocky.
"Close. The six of spades," said Judy.

"I guess I stink at card tricks."

"I know a card trick that works every time," said Judy.

"Does it have magic words?"

"Sure."

"And you'll amaze me?"

"Double sure."

"*And* you'll read my mind?"

"This trick has it *all*," said Judy.

"What's it called?"

"Let's call it . . . Red Riding Hood and the Wolf. You be Red Riding Hood and I'll be the wolf."

"Why can't *I* be the wolf?" asked Rocky.

"Fine. You be the wolf," said Judy. "I'll be Red Riding Hood. So, first Red Riding Hood goes like this. . . ."

Judy tossed all fifty-two cards up
into the air. Fifty-two cards came
raining down helter-skelter.

"Next, the wolf picks them up,"
said Judy.

"Are you cuckoo? I'm not picking
up all those cards."

"Please?" Judy asked.

"No way."

"Okay, but if you don't pick them up,
how will you do any more card tricks?"
One by one by one, Rocky picked
up all fifty-two cards. Judy cracked up.

"That's not a card trick," said Rocky.
"That's a card *prank*. A real card trick
has magic words."

"I said *please*," said Judy. "*Please* is a magic word."

"A real card trick should astound and amaze you," said Rocky.

"It *amazed me* that you picked up all fifty-two cards," said Judy.

"You didn't even read my mind," said Rocky.

"Your mind was saying you did not want to pick up all those cards. Am I right?"

Rocky stared at Judy.

"See? It worked. I got you to pick up all fifty-two cards. That's the trick."

"Hmmm. . . . You know, every good magician needs an assistant," Rocky said, smiling.

Judy grinned.

Rocky could not wait to play the new card trick on somebody. Anybody.

Judy's little brother, Stink, was karate-kicking in the Moodys' front yard.

"Hey, Stink," Judy said. "Want Rocky to show you a card trick?"

"Sure," said Stink.

"It's called Billy Goat Gruff and the Troll," said Rocky. "I'll be Billy Goat Gruff. *You* be the troll."

CHAPTER 2
The Best Backyard Magic Show Ever

Rocky had on his black top hat.

Rocky had on his long, dark cape.

Rocky got out his magic wand.

Magic show time!

Rocky looked around. The backyard was empty except for Judy Moody.

"Where is everybody?" Rocky asked Judy.

"Frank had swim practice," said Judy. "And Amy and Jessica Finch are washing pets at the humane society."

"Who ever heard of a magic show without people to watch it?" Rocky asked. "Run and get Stink."

Judy ran across the street. Rocky waited.

In no time, Judy plopped Stink onto the picnic bench in Rocky's backyard.

"I'm the only one here?" Stink asked.
"Weird."

"The Best Backyard Magic Show Ever will now begin," Rocky said in a loud voice.

"I'm not picking up cards again," said Stink. "JSYK. Just So You Know."

"No card tricks. I promise," said
Rocky. "I'm the Amazing Mr. Magic,
and this is my assistant."

"Stella the Spectacular," said Judy.

"My first trick is called the Thrill-a-fying Top Hat." Rocky pointed to the empty table covered with an old sheet.

Rocky took off his hat. Rocky set his hat on the table. He waved his magic wand over the hat.

"I will close my eyes and Judy—I mean, Stella the Spectacular—will pour water into my hat. Then, when she puts the hat back on me— ta-da!—I will not get wet."

Rocky closed his eyes. He waited for Stella the Spectacular to pour the glass of water—not *in* his hat but *behind* his hat. *Way super tricky!*

He heard Stella the Spectacular begin to pour the water.

"Hey!" yelled Stink. "She's not pouring the water in the hat."

"Am so," said Judy.

"Are not," said Stink.

"Am too," said Judy.

Rocky did not hear water being poured. He opened his eyes. He stared straight ahead at Stink.

"And now, without further ado," he said, "Stella the Spectacular will place the hat on my head. And I, the Amazing Mr. Magic, will not get wet. Not one single drop of water."

Stink cracked up. Judy shrugged. In one swoop, she put the hat on Rocky's head.

Ker-splash!

Water rushed and gushed out of
the hat. Water drenched Rocky's hair.
Water dripped down Rocky's face.

Stink fell on the ground laughing.

Rocky glared at his assistant. "Why didn't you pour the water where I told you to pour the water?" Rocky asked between clenched teeth.

"Eagle-Eyed Stink was watching me like a hawk! I had to pour it into the hat."

Rocky wiped his face on his cape.

"The show must go on," said Rocky. "For my next trick, the Amazing Mr. Magic will change this jar of peanut butter into a jar of jelly. I call it the Supersonic Switcheroo."

Rocky put the peanut-butter jar on the table. He placed a shoe box over the jar. He placed a red silk cloth over the shoe box.

Judy lifted the old sheet and hid
under the table.

"Abracadabra." Rocky tapped the red silk cloth with his magic wand. "Alla-ka-peanut-butter. Jelli-ka-zam!"

Rocky heard rustle-bustle noises under the table.

"Judy's under the table!" yelled Stink.

Rocky heard crinkle-wrinkle noises.
He smiled weakly at Stink.

At last, Judy gave him the secret
signal of three knocks from under the
table. Mr. Magic yanked off the cloth
and lifted up the shoe box.

Rocky gaped at the not-jelly jar.

Stink laughed and pointed. "That's not jelly. It's ketchup!"

Rocky poked his head under the table. "You were supposed to swap the jar of peanut butter with the jar of *jelly.*"

"I know!" said Judy. "And YOU were supposed to bring a jar of jelly, NOT a bottle of ketchup, Mr. Magic."

Rocky smacked his hand to his forehead and groaned.

"This is the worst magic show ever!" said Stink. "The Supersonic *Flub*-a-roo!"

"Quiet in the peanut gallery," said Judy.

"I'm going home," said Stink. "Unless you can pull a rabbit out of that hat or something."

"Or something," said Judy.

"You can't leave yet," said Rocky. "Those were just *practice* tricks. I will now perform the Houdini-est of all magic tricks. Mr. Magic will, before your very eyes, pull a rabbit out of this empty hat."

Stink sat back down. "For real?"

"For real," said Rocky. "See? The hat is empty." Rocky held the hat out in front of him.

Judy ducked back under the table.
Rocky heard something go *squish.*

Mr. Magic said the magic words.
"Izzy-wizzy fuzzy-wuzzy. Abiyoyo.
Alla kazam kazoo." *Kazoo* was the
secret word. *Kazoo* was the cue for Judy
to push the rabbit through the trick
bottom of the hat.

Rocky peered into the hat.

No rabbit.

"Kazoo!" he said, louder this time.

"Bless you," said Stink.

"Ka-ZOO, not ka-CHOO," said Rocky.

At last, *pop!* Rocky saw a bunny
ear poke through the bottom of the hat,
and—Zing Zang Zoom-a-roo!—he
reached into the hat and pulled out a
stuffed rabbit . . .

covered in ketchup!

"VAMPIRE RABBIT!"

Screaming, Stink leaped up and ran out of the yard. He screamed as he ran across the street. He screamed all the way inside the Moody house.

Judy came out from under the table.

Rocky's ears turned red. Rocky's face turned red.

"Sorry. I guess I sat on the ketchup," said Judy.

"Stella," said Rocky, "you are the most UN-spectacular assistant ever! You messed up all my magic tricks!"

"Not *all* of your tricks," said Judy. "One of your tricks was super-spectacular."

"It was?" Rocky asked.

"The Disappearing Pest trick," said Judy. "You made Stink disappear!"

CHAPTER 3
The Disappearing Dollar

SHAZAM! Rocky had a new magic trick.

He called Judy Moody. "Meet me at the manhole. Pronto."

Rocky ran out of his house. Judy ran out of her house. They met in the middle.

"Guess what!" Rocky told Judy. "I have a new magic trick. The best magic trick ever."

"Better than the disappearing Stink trick?" Judy asked.

"Way better," said Rocky. He stared at Judy. "Why do you have leaves in your hair?" he asked.

"I was raking leaves," said Judy. "I made one whole dollar." Judy waved a brand-spanking-new dollar bill in Rocky's face. "Want to go to the candy store?"

"I was just going to ask you if you had a dollar," said Rocky. "My new trick is called the Disappearing Dollar."

"But I get my dollar back, right?" asked Judy.

"Right," said Rocky.

Judy held out her dollar. *One whole dollar bill.* Rocky tried to take the dollar, but Judy did not let go.

"You'll get it back," said Rocky.
"Cross my heart. Magician's honor!"

At last, Judy handed over her
dollar.

"Behold!" said Rocky. "The
Amazing Mr. Magic is about to make
George Washington disappear—
poof—into thin air."

"I can't stand to watch!" said Judy.
She covered her eyes with her hands.

"You have to watch," said Rocky.

Judy uncovered her eyes. Rocky held up the dollar bill, snapping it nice and tight. "Ready? Now you see it. . . ."

Rocky crunched the dollar bill up in his hands like a gum wrapper. Judy winced.

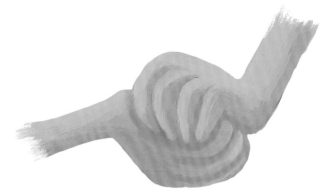

"Now you don't!" Rocky opened his hands. His hands were empty. The dollar bill was G-O-N-E, gone! *Vamoose!*

Vanished into thin air!

"Wait. What? WOW!" said Judy. "How did you do that?"

"Magic," said Rocky.

"You're like the best magician ever! But my dollar. Where is it?"

Rocky shook his head. "I can't tell you. Then it wouldn't be magic!"

"But . . . I'm Stella the Spectacular," said Judy. "Your assistant. Remember?"

"I remember that Stella messed up all of my magic tricks. This is one trick she is NOT going to mess up."

"But I'm your best friend," said Judy.

Rocky shook his head. "My lips are zipped."

"C'mon, Zipper Lips. I got three blisters for that dollar." Judy held up her hand and showed off her three Band-Aids.

"Still no," said Rocky.

"I didn't wreck your magic tricks on purpose," said Judy.

"Still no," said Rocky.

"I'm leaving," said Judy.

Rocky crossed his arms. "So leave."

"Not without my dollar."

"I already gave it back," said Rocky.

"Did not," said Judy.

"Did too," said Rocky. "Magically."

"Ugh! You know what, Rock? I take it back. You're like the *worst* magician ever. And the worst *friend* ever. You're the Amazing Mr. Meanie! *And* a big fat dollar stealer!"

Rocky watched as Judy stormed off
down the sidewalk. Boy, was she in a
mood. She jammed her hands into her
pockets. Then, Judy stopped dead in
her tracks.

Rocky waited.

At last, he saw her pull something
from her pocket. Something crinkly.
Something crumply.

Finally, Judy spun around and ran
back toward Rocky, waving her dollar
bill in the air.

"You *are* the best magician ever, Rock," she said. "You made my dollar disappear. But then you made it reappear in my pocket! And I didn't even know! Why didn't you just tell me?" she asked.

"I didn't want to spoil the magic," said Rocky.

127

Presto change-o! Rocky and Judy were friends again. *Best* friends. Magic!

Amy Namey
in Ace Reporter

For Laura

M. M.

For my mom and dad,
Felicitas and Silvano Madrid

E. M.

CONTENTS

CHAPTER 1

Did King Tut Chew Gum? 133

CHAPTER 2

Taboo 157

CHAPTER 3

Above the Fold 179

CHAPTER 1
Did King Tut Chew Gum?

Amy Namey was looking for a story. A big news story. A jump-off-the-page, super-exciting story. She walked up and down the street.

"This is Amy Namey, Ace Reporter, on the beat."

She took notes in her notebook:

11:17 Mrs. Donovan's dog barked

11:22 Mrs. Donovan's cat chased Mrs. Donovan's dog

11:37 Rocky waved from upstairs window

11:39 Mrs. Moody got her mail

"Nothing ever happens in Frog Neck Lake," Amy muttered.

"Are you talking to yourself?" asked Judy Moody, kicking a soccer ball down the street.

"Hi, Judy. I'm being a reporter, and I need a big scoop."

"A big scoop?" Judy asked. "Let's go to Screamin' Mimi's! They have tons of scoops."

"Not the ice-cream kind of scoop. The *story* kind of scoop. A big scoop is an exciting story that nobody else knows about. It's for the newspaper I'm making. C'mon over to my house."

Judy and Amy kicked the ball back and forth all the way to Amy's house.

When they got there, Judy followed Amy upstairs to her room. Amy held up her newspaper for Judy to see.

"*The Big Scoop,*" Judy read aloud. "Cool name."

Then Amy read the headlines to Judy. "*There's a New Pig in Town. Frank Pearl Wins Blue Ribbon. Rocky Zang Learns New Card Trick. Judy Moody Does* . . . something," Amy finished.

"Hey!" said Judy. "I do things! I went to college. And to Boston."

"I know! I'm not done yet," said Amy. She pointed to a big fat empty space on the front page.

"I'm saving the best story for last. Who knows? Maybe you'll be in it."

Amy's mom tapped on the door. "Hi there, Judy. Here are the papers you wanted, Ames," she said.

Amy spread the newspapers out all over her bed. "I asked my mom if I could read some of her news stories," Amy told Judy.

"*By E. Namey,*" read Judy. "Wow. Is that you?" she asked Mrs. Namey.

"That's me," said Amy's mom. "A few of my biggest stories. See?" She pointed to the top of one paper. "If your story is on page one at the top, it's a big deal. That's called *above the fold.*"

DAILY NEWS SUN TIMES

FAMOUS BRIDGE MOVED TO VIRGINIA

"Neat-o," said Judy.

"I need something mega-exciting to put above the fold on *my* paper," said Amy. "Like this." Amy read a headline: "*Girl Finds 5,000-Year-Old Gum.*"

"Rare!" said Judy.

Amy chewed the end of her pencil. "Wait a second. Maybe *we* could find a way-old piece of gum, too, or something."

"Or something," said Judy.

"Then I could write about it."

"Double rare," said Judy.

"There's a story out there," said Amy. "And I'm going to sniff it out."

"I know just the place," said Judy. "Let's go!"

"Happy sniffing," said Mrs. Namey.

"Or a shark tooth from a million years ago," said Judy.

"Or an arrowhead."

"Or an old-timey key. Or a super-duper-old coin from a way-long time ago."

"Yeah," said Amy, "like a penny that belonged to Abe Lincoln."

Amy looked at the pile of stuff they had dug up. "So far we found one marble, ten hundred rocks, one Donna Danger action figure, a rusty nail, an eraser, broken glass, a cherry pit, and three peanut shells."

"Maybe we found something old and don't even know it," said Judy, sifting through the pile. "Maybe your big scoop is right here under our noses."

Amy held up the marble. She rubbed off the dirt. "In ancient Egypt, King Tut, the Boy King, was buried with board games, right? This could be King Tut's marble."

Judy held up the eraser. "And this could be a caveman eraser. In case you make a mistake drawing your cave painting."

"Cavemen did NOT have erasers," said Amy, cracking up. "But maybe it's really a mammoth tooth. Or a dinosaur toenail?"

"Rare," said Judy. "What about this peanut shell?"

"I'm guessing . . . it could be . . . Abe Lincoln's," said Amy. "Just think— what if Abe Lincoln ate peanuts right here in *your* backyard?"

"That's a way-big-giant scoop," said Judy.

"Wait. What's this?"

Amy held up a dirt-covered lump. She blew on it.

It wasn't a nut. It wasn't a rock. It wasn't a ten-thousand-year-old cherry pit. It had teeth marks!

Amy's eyes grew wide.

Judy's eyes bugged out of her head. "Are you thinking what I'm thinking?" Judy asked.

"It's ABC gum!" said Amy. "Way-super-old, Already-Been-Chewed, Honest-to-Abe gum."

"It *looks* old," said Judy. "Did King Tut chew gum? Maybe it's three-thousand-year-old gum!"

Amy and Judy stared in awe at the way-old ABC gum.

"This is big," said Amy. "Really big."

Just then, Stink came running out the back door. He peered at the dirt-covered lump in Amy's hand. "Hey! My gum!" He snatched it and popped it into his mouth.

"Nooooooo!" Amy cried.

"Stink!" Judy shouted.

"What? It's not *that* gross," said Stink. "Just a little dirt. I was playing out here this morning and I lost my gum. I thought I swallowed it."

"There goes our three-thousand-year-old gum," said Judy.

"Hey!" said Stink, picking up the action figure. "Donna Danger! And my cat's-eye marble. And my eraser. Thanks, you guys. I thought I lost all this stuff."

"So all this stuff is Stink's?" said Amy. "Not King Tut's? Not Abe Lincoln's?"

"Sorry about your big scoop," Judy said.

"That's okay," said Amy. "I can always find King Tut's ABC gum tomorrow."

CHAPTER 2
Taboo

Amy Namey, Ace Reporter, was back on the beat. She waded ankle-deep in Frog Neck Creek behind her house.

This time, Amy Namey was monster hunting! Not the kind of monsters that live in books. Not the kind of monsters that live under the bed. The kind of monsters that live in lakes and rivers, creeks and streams.

Sea serpents! Like Nessie from Scotland!

Nabau from Borneo!

Nyami-Nyami from Africa!

"This is Amy Namey, Ace Reporter and Monster Hunter, hot on the trail of the Great Virginia Sea Serpent. Will today be the day I capture the super-secret creature on film?"

Just then, something splashed behind her.

"Aaagh!" Amy's notebook went flying. She landed bottom-first in the creek.

"What are we looking for?" said a voice. A Judy Moody voice. Amy turned and saw Judy take a bite of the baloney sandwich she was carrying.

"Judy! You scared me! Never sneak up on a reporter who's sea-monster hunting."

"Sea-monster hunting!" said Judy. "Can I help?"

"Yes. If you give me your sandwich," said Amy. "I need bait."

"Sea monsters like baloney sandwiches?" Judy asked.

"Of course they do," said Amy.

Judy handed over the sandwich. "Too bad. It has double mustard and one whole dill pickle."

"It's for a good cause," said Amy. "My mom wrote a news story about this sea serpent named Nabau, in Borneo. So I'm looking for one, too. But they're hard to find. Almost nobody gets to see one."

Judy peered into the water. "Do they look like giant snakes?" she asked.

"Some do. Like Nessie in Scotland. And Cressie in Canada. And Bessie in Lake Erie. And Tessie in Lake Tahoe. And don't forget Ogopogo!"

"O-go-WHO-go?"

"Ogopogo. It's a lake monster. It lives in Canada, along with Cressie."

"Remind me never to move to Canada," said Judy.

"I'm looking for the Great *Virginia* Sea Serpent. His name is Taboo."

"Whoa," said Judy.

"Taboo has the long neck of a dinosaur, the fins of a shark, and the tail of a giant eel. And his eyes glow in the dark. See? I drew a picture."

"Freaky-deaky," said Judy.

Just then, Amy felt something slippery, something slimy, brush against the back of her leg.

"Aaagh!" she yelled. "My leg! I felt something! Taboo!"

"Was it slippery and slimy?" Judy asked.

"Yes!"

"Did it give you the creeps?"

"Yes!"

"It was just me." Judy held up a
stick. "Hardee-har-har."

"You scared me so bad!" said Amy.

"Are you *sure* you want to find this
thing? Sounds all creepy-crawly and
swimmy-slimy to me." Judy shivered.

"How else am I going to be an Ace Reporter? First, I'm going to take a picture of Taboo. Then I'll write a story about it for my newspaper."

"Above the fold, right?" Judy asked.

Amy nodded. "Someday, I'll go around the world getting big scoops for the real newspaper. Like famous Around-the-World Reporter Nellie Bly. And my mom."

Just then, the two girls heard a giant, for-real splash. A NOT-Judy-Moody splash. They looked up the creek. They squinted into the sunlight. Water rippled over the rocks.

The two girls saw something bob up out of the water. It was riding the current. And it was heading downstream . . . right toward them!

"Do you see what I see?"

Amy gulped. "Yes. If what you see is a three-humped sea serpent with the head of a snake and the tail of an eel!"

"Do you think it smells my sandwich?" Judy asked.

But Amy wasn't listening. This was it! Her big scoop at last.

"I have to snap a picture," Amy said.

The two girls took a step closer. Amy snapped a picture. Something slippery brushed against her leg . . . *again.*

"Judy, stop touching my leg with that stick," she said.

"Stick? What stick?" said Judy. She held up both hands: empty.

Amy's heart went *thump-thump.*

"TA-BOO!" they both screamed.

They splished. They splashed. They slipped and slid.

They scrambled up the bank of the creek.

They ran across Amy's backyard.
They ran inside Amy's back door.

They ran into Amy's light, bright kitchen. "What's wrong?" asked her mom.

"Sea s-s-s-serpent!" said Amy, pointing to the creek.

"Big mon-s-s-ster!" said Judy, pointing out the back window.

"TABOO!" they both yelled.

"Phew. Close call," said Amy.

"Double phew," said Judy.

Amy held out her camera and zoomed in. She zoomed in closer.

"Hmm," her mom said. "It might be a big monster. Or it might be a big . . . imagination?"

"Mom, I saw it," said Amy.

"And don't forget we heard a big splash," said Judy.

"Girls," said Amy's mom, "do you think your sea monster just might be a three-humped tree branch?"

Amy shook her head.

"No way, no how," Judy said.

When Mrs. Namey left the kitchen, Amy turned to Judy. "This is big," she whispered. "Really big."

CHAPTER 3
Above the Fold

Amy Namey, Ace Reporter, took out the pencil from behind her ear. Amy took out her way-official notebook.

At last, she had a story. A real scoop.

Even famous Around-the-World Reporter Nellie Bly had never had a scoop this big. Nellie Bly had never spotted her very own sea monster.

Amy could not wait to write it down.

GREAT VIRGINIA SEA SERPENT SIGHTING
by Amy Namey, Ace Reporter

First there was Nessie. Then there was Nabau. Now there's Taboo. Did you know if you go monster hunting in Frog Neck Creek, you just might get mega-lucky and spot a sea monster? It's true.

Two girls from Virginia were out monster hunting this past Saturday in the Croaker Road area when they spotted something large and slimy in the creek. Eyewitness Judy Moody said, "It looked like a giant snake! No lie! It was SO not a tree branch."

If you plan to go sea-serpent hunting, take a good pair of rain boots. Need bait? Try a baloney sandwich.

And don't forget to take your camera. Taboo, the Great Virginia Sea Serpent, was captured on film. (See picture below.) Look closely. Stick? Or sea monster? You decide.

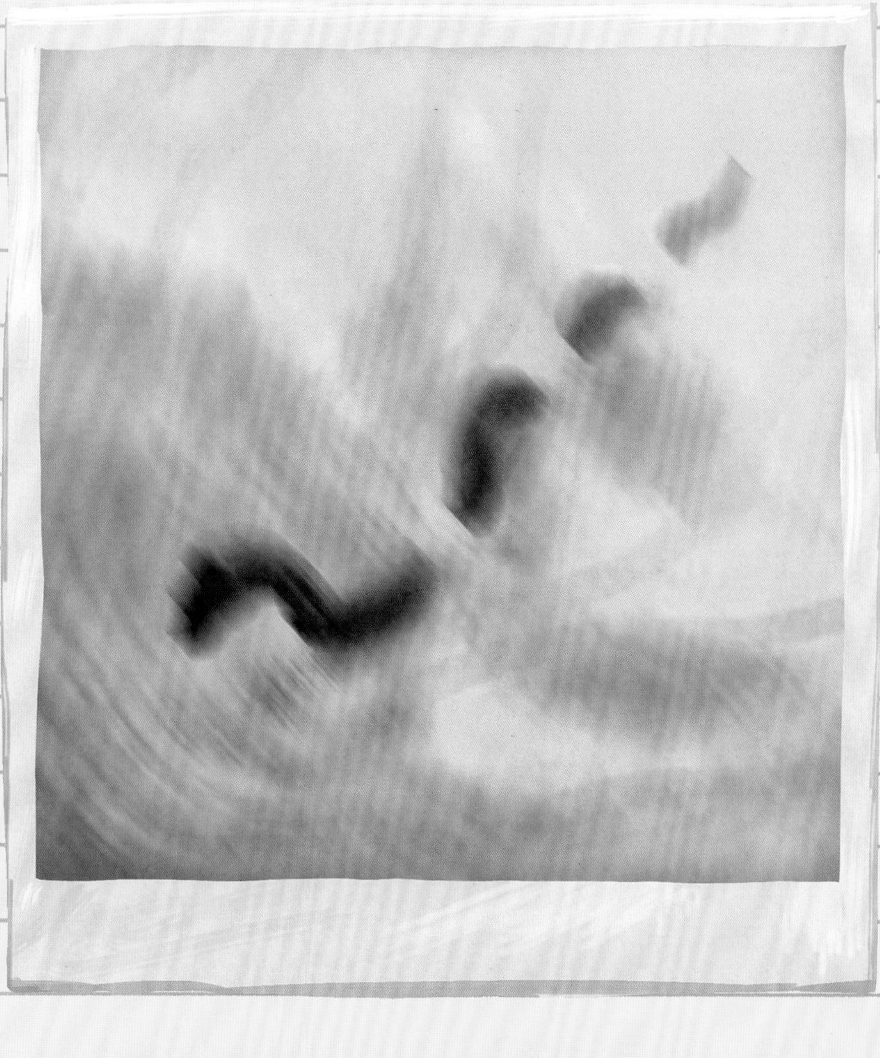

"Do you like my story?" she asked her mom, bouncing on her tiptoes.

"I love it," said her mom, giving her a squeeze. "It's exciting. It held my interest. And that ending is what we in the newspaper biz call a cliffhanger."

"Wow," said Amy. "Thanks. Wait till I show Judy!"

Amy Namey, Ace Reporter, ran down the street to Judy's house. She showed the story to Judy. She told Judy all about cliff-hangers.

"This is the best front-page above-the-fold story *ever*," said Judy.

Amy ran back home to make copies for all of her friends. "Mom! Can you help me type up my story?"

"I'm up here!" called her mom. "In your room."

Amy ran upstairs. Something about
her room was different.

A desk! Her room had a desk! An old-timey rolltop desk, right in front of the window.

"Every writer needs a desk of her own," said Amy's mom. "This desk was mine when I was a girl."

"Really?"

"Yes. It's been collecting dust up in the attic forever," said her mom. "Do you like it?"

Amy closed her eyes. She smelled the old wood. She smelled the stories. She smelled the history.

"Are you kidding?" Amy hugged her mom. "I love it to pieces!"

Amy rolled back the top of the desk. Inside were little doors and secret drawers and cubbies.

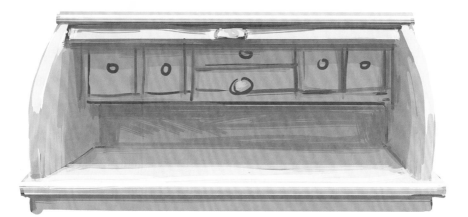

In one of the cubbies, Amy found a bunch of rolled-up papers.

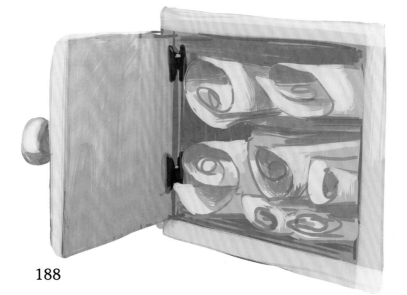

She pulled them out and unrolled them on the bed. *"The Tattle Tale,"* she read aloud.

"Oh, my old school newspapers!" said her mom. "These must be some of the first stories I ever wrote."

"Nice," said Amy.

"Here's a story I wrote about Fluffy the Rabbit, our class pet."

"Here's a poem called *Ladybug, Ladybug!*"

Together, Amy and her mother looked through all the old papers and laughed.

Later, after her mom had left
the room, Amy sat down at the old
wooden desk for the first time.

She pulled open a secret drawer.
She pulled open a tiny secret door.

Wait! Something caught Amy's eye.

Carved inside the door were some letters. Amy leaned in closer and touched each letter. They spelled a name: E-M-I-L-Y.

Her mother's name!

Amy picked up a pen. She carved three more letters into the wood, right next to her mother's: A-M-Y.

Amy was here.

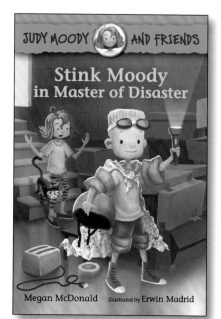